Hazel's healthy Hallowe'en

Illustrated by Kathryn Meyrick

This edition is published for Discovery Toys, Inc. by
Child's Play (International) Ltd. This edition distributed
exclusively by Discovery Toys, Inc., Martinez, CA 94553

© M. Twinn 1988   ISBN 0-85953-308-5   Printed in Singapore

Hazel was dozing
happily after
a hearty dinner.

Wake up, Hazel!
The Post Raven
is here!

Prince Boris
The Boor
invites
Hazel and
Humphrey
to the
Hallowe'en
Ball
Finest dress
please

"Yippee!
We've been invited
to the Hallowe'en Ball!"

Hazel and Humphrey dashed upstairs.

"Help! I've nothing to wear!"

Early next morning
Hazel jumped on her broom.

"To the gown shop! Quick!"

The poor old broom
could not take the strain.

"Never mind," said Humphrey.
"I'll get out the dragon cart."

After a bumpy ride
they arrived at
Felicity's gown shop.

"This is my collection
for the fuller figure,"
said Felicity.

"Now I know
why it is called
a catwalk,"
purred Humphrey.

The models did their best,
but there was nothing
in Hazel's size.

"I do want to go to the Ball,"
wailed Hazel.
"Whatever am I going to do?"

"There's only one thing to do,"
said Felicity, kindly.
"You must lose weight.

There's no magic solution.
You need a spell at the Health Farm.

And while you're there
I'll make you a dress."

Welcome, everybody.
Especially, Hazel and Humphrey.

Are you ready to begin?
That's good. Let's all join in!

Up on our toes, two, three.
Stretch our fingers, two, three.
Down, two, three.

Hazel did that 124 times.

Sway to the left, two, three.
Stretch our fingers, two, three.
Sway to the right, two, three.
Stretch our fingers, two, three.
Relax, two, three.

Hazel did that 427 times.

AT THE HEALTH FARM.

Lie flat on the floor, two, three.
Raise the left leg, two, three.
Down, two, three.
Raise the right leg, two, three.
Down, two, three.
Relax, two, three.

Hazel did that 757 times.

**Then Hazel did 934 press-ups.
She thought about food, but she
didn't get anything to eat that day.**

DAY TWO AT THE HEALTH FARM.

This morning, Hazel, we must skip and jump 2000 times.

And she did.

This afternoon, Hazel, we must cycle 10,000 miles.

And she did.

She thought about food, but she didn't get anything to eat that day.

DAY THREE AT THE HEALTH FARM.

This morning, Hazel, we must vault 800 times.

Hazel did. She dreamt of food, but she didn't get anything to eat all day.

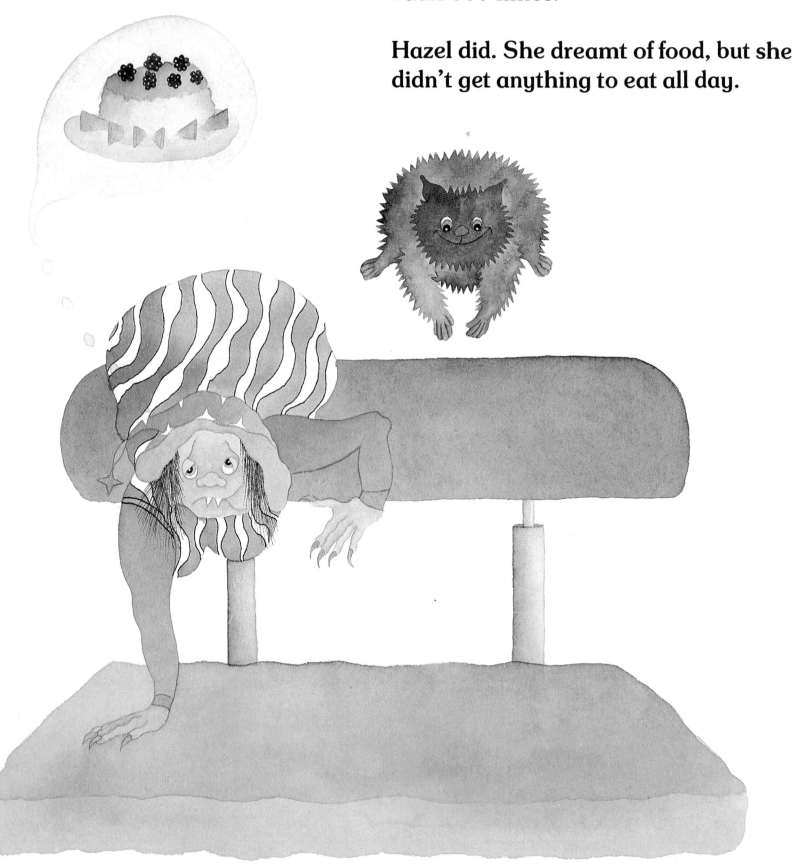

This afternoon, Hazel,
we must climb the wall bars.

Hazel climbed six mountains,
but she couldn't reach
the treat at the top.

Hazel swam 700 lengths.
She dreamt of food but she
only swallowed water that day.

TRICK OR TREAT RACE

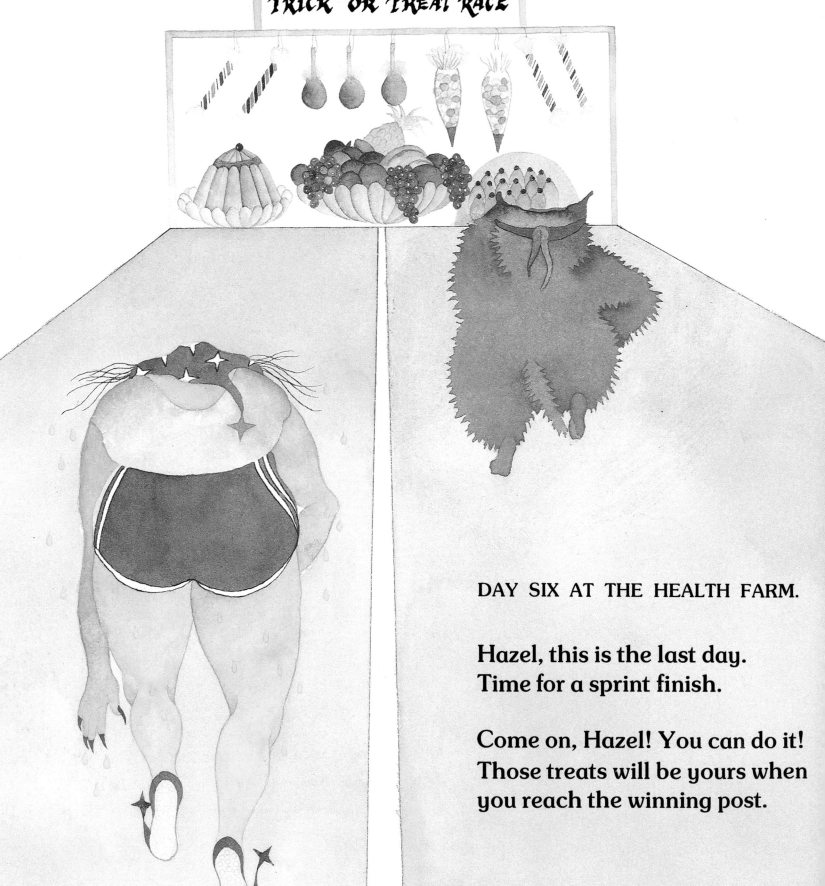

DAY SIX AT THE HEALTH FARM.

Hazel, this is the last day.
Time for a sprint finish.

Come on, Hazel! You can do it!
Those treats will be yours when
you reach the winning post.

"Uggh! Cardboard!
I give in!"

No need, Hazel. You've won.
You're thin!

Hallowe'en at last!
It has all been worthwhile.
Hazel and Humphrey
arrived in style.

Hazel was greeted
by Boris the Boor.
He'd never seen Hazel
so lovely before.

"Hazel, you look serene,
fit to be a fairy queen.
This could be the start
of a fine romance.
May I have the pleasure
of this dance?"

Gentle reader, if this is
the end you've been waiting for,
Close the book
and read no more.

"I didn't go to all this trouble for a silly man."

And Hazel made a dash
for the spread.

Hazel, what manners!
Don't you care?
And look, your dress
is beginning to tear.

"Dear friends, I'm sorry.
It's no use pretending.

This is what I call
a happy ending."

DAY FOUR AT THE HEALTH FARM.

Today we will swing
over a muddy ditch.

Hazel succeeded 499 times.
Then she fell in.

DAY FIVE AT THE HEALTH FARM.

We'll spend today in the pool.

Bravely, Hazel took the plunge.

Humphrey wished he was a dog
and began to look like one.